HOW CHEETAH GOT HIS TEARS

Written by Avril van der Merwe

Illustrated by Heidi-Kate Greeff

AUTHOR'S DEDICATION
This book is dedicated to the memory of my friend Rose Baker,
the former principal of Edgemead Pre-Primary School and
Garden Village Pre-Primary School, in tribute to our shared
love of children, books, the arts, animals, travel and adventure.

On a breezy day, Cheetah loved to stalk through the long African grass.
On a sunny day, Cheetah loved to sit high on a rock watching over the plains of Africa.
On a rainy day, Cheetah loved to crouch under the branches of a leafy tree.
But on any kind of day, Cheetah loved to run. Most of all, he loved
to run. Every day Cheetah practised his running. Every day
he ran faster and faster, until at last he was sure he
could run faster than any other animal on earth.

'I am the fastest in the world!' he boasted, sitting on top of his favourite rock and puffing out his chest, 'I am the king of runners!'

Lion growled. 'I am king of the beasts. You are not the king of anything! You don't even know how to roar!'

Elephant trumpeted in agreement. 'I am much bigger than you. I am the biggest of all. You are too skinny to be a king, Cheetah!'

Rhinoceros snorted. 'I'll poke you with my horn and toss you into a thorn bush, Cheetah. Then we'll see who's king!'

Giraffe plucked a leaf from the top of the thorn tree and munched it thoughtfully. 'I have the longest legs,' she said, 'I'm sure I must be the fastest.'

From his perch on a branch in the tree, Monkey chuckled. 'Hah, Cheetah! You can't scamper up a tree like me! What kind of king is that?'

Antelope was staying as far away as she could from Lion and Cheetah. From her hiding place behind Elephant she whispered, 'Yes, Cheetah, I can also run very fast and I can jump very high, but I don't go around calling myself king!'

At this Lion and Cheetah turned to stare hard at Antelope. She huddled closer to Elephant for protection.

Cheetah sneered, 'Hey Lion,
let's both chase Antelope! The one
who runs fastest and catches her first
will be the winner!'

'No you don't!' rumbled Elephant,
standing protectively over Antelope.
He swung his trunk at Cheetah.
'Nobody is chasing Antelope today.'

'See, Cheetah,' laughed Hyena,
'You are no king.'

'I'll prove it,' whined Cheetah.
'Race me, and I'll prove it!'

The other animals looked at each other. Cheetah was fast, very fast. They watched him run every day.

But before they could say anything, Cheetah quickly added, 'I'll race you from this rock to the fever tree. Hoopoe bird can start us off.'

The animals looked towards the fever tree.
It did not seem too far away.
Maybe one of them would be able to beat Cheetah after all.

Without saying another word, the animals lined up for the race.
First Cheetah, then Lion, then Elephant, and then Rhinoceros.
Last to line up were Giraffe, Antelope and Monkey,
standing closely together and as far away as
they could get from Cheetah and Lion.

'Hoop!' called Hoopoe bird.
'Hoop, hoop, go!'

In a swirl of dust, the animals set off at top speed.

Lion rushed along using his powerful muscles and sharp claws.
Elephant's huge legs thumped so hard they made the ground
shake like an earthquake.
Rhinoceros snorted with effort, his little tail quivering from
side to side as his short legs hurried as fast as they could.
Giraffe set off at an easy run, her long neck swaying in
time with her long legs.
Antelope raced along, leaping gracefully
into the air as she went.
Monkey scampered on all fours,
chattering encouragement to
himself as he ran.

Hyena did not run at all, but rolled around in the dust, laughing at the sight of the animals trying to outrun Cheetah. He did not care who was king, as long as he was not the one who had to do any work. 'Look at them trying so hard,' he chuckled to himself. 'They should just enjoy an easy life like me, stealing other animals' food and basking in the sun.'

From the moment that Hoopoe bird called 'Go!' it was Cheetah who leaped ahead of the others in an instant, and he was already waiting, panting, at the fever tree when, one by one, they skidded to a stop there in a cloud of dust.

'Ha! Ha!' he jeered, 'I told you! I'm the fastest runner of all! I'm the king of running! I can even run faster than Wind!'

The other animals watched him in sulky silence, trying to think of something that would stop Cheetah's noisy boasting.

A sudden gust of wind rattled the leaves in the tree above their heads.

'Race me then, Cheetah!' cried Wind, 'Race me, if you can!'

'Don't be silly,' snarled Cheetah, 'How can I race you? I can't even see you. Nobody can see you, Wind. And if we can't see you, how can we tell who wins?'

'Are you afraid?' mocked Wind,
'Are you a scaredy-cat?'

Cheetah hissed and spat. 'I'm no scaredy-cat!
I am the king of runners!'

'Well then,' taunted Wind, 'Race me if you can!'

'Go on Cheetah!' called the other animals,
'Run and race Wind!'

Cheetah swished his tail in anger. If he refused Wind's challenge, everyone would laugh at him for being scared of losing.
Then he had an idea. He knew that Wind could not change direction as quickly as he could. Usually Wind blew in one direction for a long time before it turned around and came back again. He would trick Wind into a race that Wind could not win.

'All right!' he snarled, 'I will race you, Wind. I will race you to the thorn tree and back again.'

'I'll start you off,' offered Elephant.

Cheetah gazed back to the thorn tree near
the rock where the animals had begun the first race.

'I'm ready,' he said. 'I'm ready to race Wind and win!'

'On your marks,' bellowed Elephant, 'Get set...' Cheetah waited.

Elephant raised his trunk and trumpeted so loudly that Cheetah
was startled and shot off like an arrow towards the thorn tree.

'Go Cheetah!' shouted the animals, 'Run faster than Wind!'

Wind blew.

Wind howled.

Wind roared.

Wind blew and howled and roared so hard that the trees bent low and the branches swayed.

'Look!' cried the animals, 'Look! Wind has reached the thorn tree before Cheetah! Wind is winning!'

'The race isn't over,' panted Cheetah,
'We have to turn around and go back again!'

Cheetah skidded all the way around the
thorn tree and set off at top speed
back towards the fever tree.

Still Wind blew.

It blew so hard that Cheetah's small ears were blown flat against his head.

It blew so hard that Cheetah's tail was blown out behind him as straight as a spear.

It blew so hard that it stung Cheetah's eyes until tears started pouring down his cheeks, and he could no longer see where he was going.

Cheetah shook his head to shake the tears away, but still they kept streaming down. He turned this way and that to try to get Wind out of his eyes, but still his eyes stung and his tears ran.

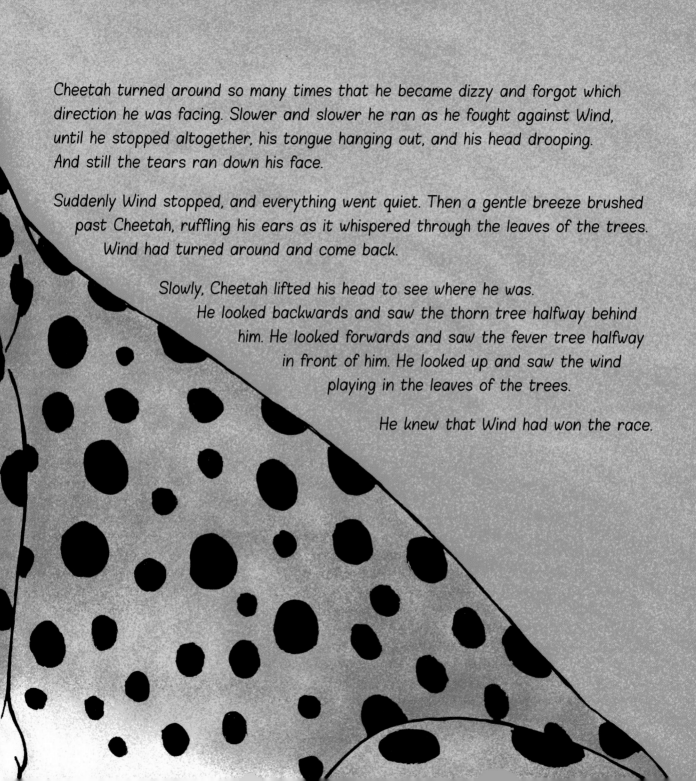

Cheetah turned around so many times that he became dizzy and forgot which direction he was facing. Slower and slower he ran as he fought against Wind, until he stopped altogether, his tongue hanging out, and his head drooping. And still the tears ran down his face.

Suddenly Wind stopped, and everything went quiet. Then a gentle breeze brushed past Cheetah, ruffling his ears as it whispered through the leaves of the trees. Wind had turned around and come back.

Slowly, Cheetah lifted his head to see where he was. He looked backwards and saw the thorn tree halfway behind him. He looked forwards and saw the fever tree halfway in front of him. He looked up and saw the wind playing in the leaves of the trees.

He knew that Wind had won the race.

He looked at the other animals, expecting them to laugh at him, but they didn't.

Lion padded softly over and sat in front of Cheetah. Elephant lumbered closer and stood next to Lion. Rhinoceros shuffled towards him and stopped alongside Elephant.

Giraffe walked over and stood beside
Rhinoceros, bending her long neck
down towards Cheetah.

Antelope hesitated,
then pranced closer,
edging herself between
Elephant and Rhinoceros.
In a skip and a jump, Monkey landed
on Elephant's back, and scurried to sit
between Elephant's ears.
Even Hyena slunk closer, but not too close.
They all looked at Cheetah, feeling sorry for him
because the tears still ran down his face.

'Cheetah,' Lion grunted softly, 'You are very fast. You can run from the thorn tree to the fever tree faster than all of us. But you cannot run very far or for very long. And you cannot run faster than Wind. I am sorry, but you are not the king.'

Lion reached over and patted Cheetah on the cheek with his paw.
Elephant stretched out his trunk and blew softly across Cheetah's back.
Rhinoceros huffed and stirred up the dust with his front legs.
Giraffe leaned even further down and flicked Cheetah's ears with her tongue.
Antelope batted her long eyelashes at Cheetah from where she stood.
Monkey chattered gently at Cheetah from his perch on Elephant's neck. 'But we do admire you, Cheetah, we really do. You are handsome and fit and lean and fast, so very fast, even if you cannot climb trees.'

Still Cheetah's tears ran down his cheeks. They ran because his eyes still stung from the fierce blowing of Wind. But most of all they ran because the animals were being so kind to him when he did not deserve it.

'Thank you,' he said, 'Thank all of you. Even you, Antelope.'

Antelope shrank back between Elephant and Rhinoceros. She would rather not have any attention drawn to her.

'I will never forget this day,' said Cheetah.

And to prove that he has not forgotten, his tears have run down his cheeks from that day to this, and have never stopped.

Published in 2017 by Puffin Books
an imprint of Penguin Random House South Africa (Pty) Ltd
Company Reg. No. 1953/000441/07
The Estuaries, 4 Oxbow Crescent, Century Avenue, Century City 7441, Cape Town, South Africa
PO Box 1144, Cape Town, 8000, South Africa
www.penguinrandomhouse.co.za

PUBLISHER: Linda de Villiers
MANAGING EDITOR: Cecilia Barfield
DESIGN MANAGER: Beverley Dodd
DESIGNER: Helen Henn
EDITOR: Gill Gordon
Reproduction by Hirt & Carter Cape (Pty) Ltd
Printed and bound in Malaysia by Times Offset (M) Sdn Bhd

ISBN 978-1-48590-034-4

This book is printed on FSC®-certified paper.
Forest Stewardship Council® (FSC®) is an independent
international non-governmental organization.
Its aim is to support environmentally sustainable,
socially and economically responsible
global forest management.